I0553604

The Big Ideas Club Presents

Living Myths

Revisiting Ancient Greece

Wolfish Rage I:

The City is Sick

By

Jason Kassel, PhD

Recursive Publishing

Part I: The City is Sick

Is This a Child's Lesson?

Deicoon

A group of twenty well-dressed old men march together up a mountain hill and towards Hercules' home. Immediately ahead of them, Hercules' wife, Megara, walks holding her youngest son - Therimachus - in her arms. Her left hand grasps the middle son - Creontiades. The eldest - Deicoon - grasps onto her skirt. In front of them, Hercules' old father hunches over a cane and struggles with his climb. The five members of Hercules' family are disheveled and dirty. When the entire group reaches the top of the hill, they arrive at the large outer courtyard of Hercules' home.

His grandfather faces his old friends. "Everybody knows my name."

Deicoon feels the dirty fabric, smells his mother's sweaty fear, and sees her shaking with tears. He wishes he could calm her but his own heart races and his thoughts are scattered. He tries to listen to his grandfather tell his old friends about their family history.

Grandfather continues to talk about all that Zeus did and how he is responsible for father's birth. He talks about the dragon's teeth from which the Thebens were born. Why are these dragon people not helping us?

His grandfather's voice quakes in despair. "Remember their wedding?" He reminisces about the day father and mother wed. "On their wedding day, my new daughter-in-law was escorted by all the people of Thebes. Everyone sang songs and played lutes as my son, the glorious hero, led her to my house as his bride."

Why did father have to abandon mother and the rest of us? He left us in the care of grandfather who has done what he can but he has no respect among the young and powerful. Look at all these old men. Where are the ones who can help? Where are the family friends? Every day I've been told how much these people owe my father and our family. I've been fed stories about the labors my father has done and how he has brought calm to the land. Is this how people in Thebes say thank you? Is this a child's lesson?

"I think Hera hatched the plan but it may be Hercules' fate." His grandfather finds a place to sit down. "The last time anyone saw my son Hercules was when he passed through the mouth of Taenarum down into Hades." He puffed his chest proudly. "He is going to drag the three-bodied dog Cerberus into the earth's light."

Grandfather continues to sing my father's praises even though he has abandoned us.

He looks up to see his mother with her arms wrapped around his youngest brother. She holds him tightly to her bosom but Therimachus won't stop crying. She tries to sing a lullaby to soothe her child's heart. It does no good because her own heart beats too fast and the infant senses fear.

Grandfather talks of politics. This man Lykos is a tyrant who murdered old king Creon and stole the throne. That's why we suffer. Grandfather has taught me that the new king is a foreigner from Euboea. He brought civil strife and dissension to Thebes. Our family's connection to Creon has become a curse. Father has abandoned us to perform another of his labors in the bowels of the underworld. He has left us here alone with an old man for protection. This new tyrant king wants to kill all of us because of fear. He knows we will avenge our family's murder.

His grandfather continues to address his group of old comrades. He looks around his mother to see his brother by her side. He is proud to see that even at his young age his brother knows to show the world courage.

"I am here at the Altar of Zeus," his grandfather implores his old and powerless friends. "I stand with his wife to tend and guard his children. My son, Hercules himself, established this monument to commemorate his great victory over the Minyae."

Grandfather, if this victory is so great, why aren't the young and powerful men of Thebes helping us?

"We have been locked out of our house and are here at this altar without food, drink, clothes or anything but the earth below." His grandfather goes on with the old men as though they have any ability to do anything about it. "They have locked us out and no one will help. Our powerful friends have proven insincere and left us. Our true friends are powerless to help." His grandfather walks around the group hugging his old friends. "The gods bring such misfortune to us mortals. If anyone helps us, may they be free of these mortal burdens."

His mother, weeping and trembling uncontrollably, falls to her knees on the ground. Facing Zeus' temple, she places Creontidas on the ground, and holds both hands high. "Old man," she speaks to grandfather. "You were a famous warrior who led Cadmeian troops against the Taphians and took their city. Where is your reward?" She falls face forward to the ground and Deicoon has to quickly sweep up his brother before his mother rolls her entire weight on his head.

"How do mortals remember your deeds?" If Deicoon's mother were a child, her behavior would resemble a child's tantrum with her arms and legs flailing. "Fortune gave me a king for a father and people said he was blessed because he was rich." She forces herself to her knees to face the idol of Zeus. "What did my father's blessedness, wealth, and throne bring? Men who hurled long spears at him." She falls again. "Men always act this way because they are jealous of those blessed with prosperity." She turns with her face toward the sky. "And father was blessed with happy children. Including me, who was given to Hercules as a lawful bride."

His mother rises, does her best to calm herself, and tries to stop her weeping. "All that good fortune is gone." She can't stop her weeping. "Good fortune flew away." She walks to his grandfather, throws her arms around his neck, and her wet tears flow like a river on his shoulder. "You and I, these boys, all of us are going to be killed."

While watching his mother behave this way, Deicoon stood holding his infant brother. His younger brother's outward bravery disappeared and he ran to Deicoon's side. When they heard the word killed, they ran to their mother and clutched her tattered and dirty dress.

"Look at my children huddled under my wings like chicks protected by their mother."

Why is this happening to us? Where is father? Why did he abandon us and leave Thebes? Will he ever return? Mother has told stories but I see in her face and eyes she doesn't believe them herself. Oh, where is my father? Will I ever touch his knees again?

His mother has again fallen on her knees begging Zeus' idol. His grandfather's old friends shift uncomfortably and look away as his mother speaks. Facing Zeus she speaks to his grandfather. "Tell me, old man, what can we do? What is the solution? You're our only hope."

Grandfather and mother spoke last night about running away from Thebes. I heard them say the tyrant king's soldiers are everywhere. They are guarding every path out of this city and won't even let us humiliate ourselves and run away. This tyrant king hates my family and knows we three sons will seek revenge.

It kills Deicoon inside to see mother act and speak this way on her knees. "Speak truthfully, old man. Tell me how to prepare for my death."

His grandfather lifts his mother. "I need time to think before offering advice."

"Old man, do you love life so much you want to spend your time being miserable?"

Mother, such terrible things to say. Is there really no hope for us?

"Yes, I love life and cling to its hopes."

"I love hope but this is hopeless."

Mother!

"One remedy is to postpone the misery."

"The time before the remedy appears is when the misery bites most fiercely."

Deicoon looks at his brother who's clinging to his mother's skirt.

These words she speaks, they terrify me. Last night, grandfather told me the longer it takes for father to return the better. It means there is still hope and opportunity for him to return. Who do I trust? Mother or grandfather?

His grandfather collects all three grandsons into a group. Deicoon does what he can to steady his mother. He hears his grandfather whisper into his mother's ear. "Stay calm. Use your sweet words to trick your sons and stop their tears. Remember, the winds vary in force from moment to moment and so do the winds of human misery."

His grandfather places his hands of Deicoon's shoulders and slowly lowers himself so that he is face-to-face and eye-to-eye with his grandson. "The force of winds will subside and everything will separate.

One extreme will change to another. The brave trust hope and the cowards despair. "

Ancient Palsied Legs

Among the group of twenty old men are two members of Amphytrion's old battalion that led the successful charge against the Taphians. They shuffle about and avoid eye contact with one another. They walked the hill and arrived at Zeus' temple together, arm in arm. Over time, watching Megara display her spectacle and their honorable old friend debase himself, they drifted apart. They couldn't bear the thought of physical intimacy during such a terrible time.

His old sergeant stares at his feet and kicks the ground.

Here I stand, the glorious feared warrior of Greece. Hunched over a walking stick. I stand inside

Zeus' high-roofed palace singing sad songs, dirges, and lamentations.

For the view of the world, the sergeant shows an air of noble unease and discomfort. It is an embarrassing spectacle to see old honorable friends behave in such a way. Inside, though, he weeps.

I am nothing. An old gray bird. A voice. A ghost. A dark vision from an old sleep.

On the other side of Zeus' temple, Amphytrion's former captain of the guards shuffles his feet. He barely makes eye contact with a single friend before lowering his head. He too shows the world noble disgrace at the sight of an old friend's shame.

I am old and my ancient legs are palsied. I want to help the fatherless sons and my poor old friend. How awful for the mother. If only I were young again. I fought in, and won, glorious wars. If I were young, I would pick up a spear and shield for you and your grandchildren. Look at how the boys' eyes flash with both anger and fear. They are their father's children.

Doesn't this tyrant king know Hercules is loved

throughout Greece? If the Theban people allow his

sons to die, how many allies will Greece lose?

The old men's painful reveries are interrupted by a bugle's sound. The notes signal the arrival of King Lykos and his men.

Why Prolong Your Miserable Lives?

King Lúkos steps onto the soil of Zeus' temple. He stands before the altar with his two armed guards and stares at the crowd. As he walked up the mountain's hill, he knew the citizens of Thebes distrusted and feared him. The thoughts pleased him. Ever since Nycteus appointed him regent of Thebes, Lykos has used his power to create dissension and civil strife to decenter Thebes. He brought these diseases with him when he settled in King Pentheus' land.

How could Thebans know what fate had in store when Lykos settled in their land? They had no idea that Polydorus would die or that Nycteus would serve as Labdacus' regent. How could they have known that Zeus would impregnate Nycteus' daughter, Antiope, and she would carry his twins - Amphion and Zethus? Could Thebans have known Nycteus would die of wounds? Who could have foretold that Lykos would use his war-making skills to attack and kill Epopeus in order to punish Antiope?

When Epopeus died, his cowardly heir Lamedon gave Antiope to Lykos. Lykos made the fateful decision at Mount Cithaeron to abandon the twins and left them with shepherds. Once he gained custody of Antiope, Dirce locked her up, and tortured her mercilessly. After many years, Antiope escaped and found her twins. They vowed to avenge their mother's punishment and returned to Thebes intent on killing Lykos and Dirce. They were ready but, in a dream, Hermes appeared and the twins were forbidden from killing Lykos.

The twins, however, have remained a scourge on his land. They continually stole his gold from his banks and stores from his grainery. He has learned the lesson of blood vengeance and sworn a vow to never let his enemies' children live again.

Looking at the old men, he shakes his head in disgust. Without any emotion except the pleasure of killing an enemy, Lykos' steely eyes gaze over the dirty and tattered clothes worn by Amphitryon, Megara and the three boys.

"I have a question and since I am your King you must answer." His strong accent makes his speech barely perceptible to his old and ashamed audience. They have to walk toward the guards and listen to their translations. "How much longer do you want to stay alive? What hope do you see? Why prolong your miserable lives?" He walks around Zeus' soil and looks the idols over from earth to heaven. "Do you think Zeus will save you from your death?" He laughs. "Do you think Hercules will return and protect his sons?"

King Lykos walks to the three boys who are huddling at their mother's tattered and dirty skirt. He puts his hands under the chin of the one he assumes is oldest. "Your father is dead in the halls of Hades below." He smiles as the boy eyes water and then disperse tears. "Do you really think he's coming back from down there?" He lets go of the boy's chin and walks to the old grandfather.

"Amphitryon, a woman moans and groans about death. Why are you afraid of death? Aren't you a friend of Zues?" The king laughs and spits on Zeus' soil. "Haven't you all heard?" He raises his voice, looks at the old men, and smiles as they stand near his guards trying to understand his words. "Throughout the whole of Greece, this man has traveled and told everyone who would listen that Zeus cuckolded his wife." Lykos laughs a hearty laugh and looks at the old men. "This woman tells everyone her husband is earth's greatest hero." He shakes his head and, again, spits on Zeus' soil. "Hercules killed a snake and lion. Greece believed the words your son spoke. His words were untrue. He told a story and caught the whole of your people in a snare."

King Lykos walks toward his guards who are surrounded by old men. "You Thebans believed Hercules when he said caught these animals with his bare hands. Hercules is not a man who will save you from your death." He turns and walks toward Amphitryon. "Old man, there are no more excuses. I will not wait any longer. It is time for your grandsons to be put to death."

Hercules Uses A Bow And Arrow

King Lykos walks to Zeus' idol and places his hand on the marble. "Hercules may have been a courageous hunter but he is no warrior." Touching Zeus' idol, he looks at each of the old men. "Hercules is a coward. He never strapped a shield to his arm or went eye-to-eye with a man holding a spear." He pats the marble of Zeus' idol and spits again on Zeus' soil. "Hercules uses a bow and arrow which everyone knows are a coward's weapon. What courage does it take to use a bow?" He walks to one of his guardsmen and places his fist around his spear. He lifts the spear over his head. "Courage comes from using a spear and standing your ground." He pounds his chest with his spear hand. "That's courage! That's bravery!"

Caught up in his war passions, King Lykos stands silently staring at his spear. He tosses it to his guard and faces Amphitryon. "Old man, don't think

I'm cruel. I know I sit on the throne because I killed Megara's father Creon." Lykos places an arm on Amphitryon's shoulder, moves his mouth next to Amphitryon's ear, and whispers. "If I allow these boys to grow, they will seek revenge."

Protect These Children

Look at this old man. He stands with his arms raised and appeals to his god Zeus. What a fool. Listen to him talk about how heroic men use a bow and arrow. This man who is supposed to be such a warrior is talking about a bow and arrow. This all makes me laugh. This is taking too long, I need to return to the throne room. I have a meeting with the master of coins. I am going to call in debts and enhance the civil strife. The more sickness this city breeds the stronger I become.

"Old man, what are you ranting about?"

"You better listen, you tyrant." The old man sputters and curses his king who snorts in reply. "Go back to Euboa and ask them about my son's bravery. That is your country, that is where you are from. Do they sing your praises there? What brave deeds have you executed in your own country?"

This old man should lower his voice. My guards should not be hearing such things.

King Lykos stands still and quiet and listens to the pathetic old man rant about the bow and arrow. The old man spits his convoluted logic into the air.

How much fun this is. Watching this old man debase and humiliate himself. I will kill his grandsons as he stands watching helplessly. What does this old man think he gains by cursing my name and hurling insults? I'll let him rant and rave then provide punishment.

"We are better than you." The old man whines to the sky. "We should be delivering this fate to you."

This old man insults me and now he's whining about allowing them to go into exile. After all his cursing, he's asking me for a favor.

"Be careful the winds of fortune don't veer round and send violence in your direction."

The old man turns toward the old Thebans. He raises his right arm and turns in a circle. "Everyone who lives in the land of Cadmus. I accuse you of having failed Hercules' sons. You disgrace yourselves." The old man lowers his arm, and his old body crumbles. "You betray the man who saved Thebes when he faced the Minyan army."

Why does this old man talk of praise? This country is meant to be ruled and plundered. Who cares about these stories of glory and acts of bravery. Why does this old man think the families of Thebes will provide protection? Is he really talking of repayment? This old man has learned nothing of the behavior of the mortal men in the land of Thebes.

"Why won't Thebes or Greece protect these children?" The old man walks to his grandsons and holds and huddles with the eldest. "Poor boys, all you see is a weak old man. I love you so much, but I have nothing more than a noisy tongue." The old man does his best to stand upright. "If only you boys had seen me in my youth." The old man transforms his body and approximates youth. "What vigor, what strength I had. My knees were once so strong and now age makes them quake."

The old man turns toward Lykos, balls his hand into a fist, and shakes it in front of the king's face. "In my youth, I was so strong. Look at me now, I am weak with age. If I was young and strong, though, I would grab a spear and soak you in your own red blood." His balled fist still in the king's face, the old man turns to face the group of old men. "If I were young again, I would watch as this coward flees beyond the pillars of Atlas."

One of the old men speaks loudly. "Amphitryon, please, say something nice about the king before it is too late."

Is he done? Is it my turn to speak?

Lykos nods his chin toward his guards and one of them places the old man in a bear hug. "Insult me all you want, old man. Watch how I repay your harsh words with even harsher deeds."

Lykos looks at his other guard. "Send wood-cutters Helicon and the valleys of Parnassus and cut logs of oak. Bring the logs to this altar, pile up a stack of wood all round the altar, and set it on fire." He rubs his hands together and smiles. "Burn this family alive. Teach the people of Thebes that I am king and the dead no longer rule this land."

The guard releases the old man, the two salute, and they walk off. Pleased with the power he wields, Lykos turns toward the old man. "Want to keep talking, old man? I will not only kill Hercules' sons, I will also burn your palace. One disaster after another will remind you that you are slaves and I am King.”

We Are Too Old

The group of twenty old men, standing near the foreign tyrant's guards, feel shame and humiliation. They have no words. A group of five old men walk to the edge of the hill and look down on the city below Zeus' temple.

One old man looks at another. “Where are the young men of Thebes? This city used to give birth to men of Ares, the god of war. Young men used to be from the teeth of dragons.”

The other old man shakes his head in despair and speaks in a hushed tone. “The young men won't help you and I smash this foreigner's godless skull to a bloody pulp. Civil strife and dissension make Thebes weak.”

"How can the young men of Thebes carry those big sticks and not use them?"

Another old man joins the conversation. "Thebes suffers from the political disease of dissension and civil strife. The young are enslaved and act shamefully."

"Will we let this brutal tyrant steal our toil and reap our harvest?"

The men huddle together in a tight group and whisper. "I curse this tyrant and no longer take his orders."

"Yes, he must go."

"Back to that horrible foreign land of his."

"He should tell his own people what to do." All of the men in the tight, whispering huddle nod their heads.

"Go, you awful tyrant. Leave Thebes."

"As long as I'm alive, I will protect Hercules' sons while he is deep beneath the earth." An old man, leaning heavily on a walking stick, speaks in a barely heard whisper. "Under this tyrant king's possession the land has become ruined with disease. He became king without rewarding Hercules, the city's benefactor."

An old man, who had not yet spoken, but had puffed up chest while listening, became visibly deflated. "Wait a second. Have we forgotten? We are nothing but old men."

An old man who had been leading the whispers lowered his chest. "Yes, you are right."

"We take on too much."

"If I were young."

The old men nod in unison. "Yes, of course. If we were young, our right hands would hold spears and fight."

"Absolutely."

An old man lowers his head in shame. "But we are too old."

"Old and weak."

An old man separates himself from the huddle, walks to the edge of the hill, and looks down on the city below. "Young men of Thebes, where are you?"

"If I was young, I'd puff myself up and do a glorious deed."

"Look down there." The group of old men stand in a line looking down. "Our citizens and our city are diseased. The city of Thebes is sick with dissension and civil strife."

"Once our young men called the foreigner King Lykos, they became his slaves."

An old man speaks in a loud voice. "Thebes is sick with the disease of dissension and civil strife."

Act With Virtue

The children's mother, wife to Hercules, and daughter-in-law to Amphytryon has watched the king harass and threaten her children in silence. As the king was berating Amphitryon, she drifted towards the huddled group of old men, and did her best to listen to their whispers.

These old men are so kind with their words. But I worry for them. If the king should hear their virtuous indignation and anger regarding our injustice, I fear the tyrant will vent his anger and punish them.

She walks toward her father-in-law and tries to reason with him. "Amphitryon, please listen to what I'm about to say and speak if you think I make sense." She finds a bench to sit on and looks at her three boys trembling together. The eldest holds the infant in his arms while the middle child's eyes reveal stark terror. "Father-in-law, how can I risk such a painful ending for the lives I labored to bring forth. Fate has decided it is time to die and, yes, death is a dreadful fate." She places her hands in his and squeezes tightly. "Why should we provide food for our enemy's banquet? They are going to torture us with fire and laugh while watching us burn alive." Tears well in her eyes. "The thought of that shame is worse than death." Tears flow down her cheeks and she places her head on Amphytryon's shoulder.

She composes herself. "Amphytryon, we must act with virtue while standing in the palace of Zeus."

Look at the old man's face. Is my father-in-law a coward in his old age? What about the tales of his heroic and glorious battlefield acts? Does he desire a coward's death?

She grasps Amphytryon's hands tightly. "My husband's reputation as a brave and virtuous man is at stake. If his children die a coward's death, they will carry the stain of cowardice." She looks her father-in-law in the eyes. "You know that would afflict their parents with disgrace. I must act bravely as well. A wife's actions must match her husband's."

Hercules wouldn't choose a coward's death and neither will I.

"Amphitryon, I have weighed your message of hope. I no longer hold on to hope's hand." She turns so Amphitryon stares at her back. He reaches to touch her but she moves away. "Hercules will not return from the world of the dead below the earth. No one has ever returned from Hades' halls." She faces him. "Do you think this tyrant will soften because of words? Friendly overtures will not work on him. He is too stupid to make concessions or yield in any way."

Before he left Hercules taught me this wisdom. He explained that only wise and noble men, men of breeding and wisdom, have a sense of decency and mercy.

"Father-in-law, I too had thought of exile. But to die in a foreign land? Our host's faces would look sweetly at banished friends and smile for a single day. Then we will die in abject poverty." Again, she leans against his body. "That is a fate as miserable as death."

I will be brave for my sons. It is my lot to prepare my children for their death. This is my fate.

"Old man, your blood is in my sons' veins and your bravery courses through their arms. It does no good to struggle against the gods, mortals can't escape our destiny. Your fighting spirit is foolish because fate has already decided." She stands and looks at Zeus' idol. "No one is able to alter the events that must take place."

The old men approach her father-in-law and grab onto him.

Listen to these old men talk about their youthful glories. They all have memories of brave, strong, heroic arms but they only offer old and useless ones today. Still, their words are welcome and kind. They are comforting.

One of the old men is staring at her children. "What will Fate deliver?"

Her father-in-law speaks to his friends but his words are addressed to her. "I don't care about my reputation as a hero or coward. I don't care about my life. My only wish, and it may be a vain hope, is to save my grandchildren."

He separates from his friends and walks towards Lykos.

Oh, my father-in-law still has his bravery. Yes, kill both of us but do it first. Please don't make me bear witness to the sight of my sons gasping their dying breaths. Please don't make me plead while watching them burn.

"Other than that, do as you wish." The old man lowers his head in shame. "We have no defense."

She rushes to the king's side, touches the fabric of his robe, and falls to her knees. "I beg one other favor, a double kindness. Unlock the doors of Zeus' temple so that we may go inside and dress the children in funeral robes." She clasps her hands together and beseeches him. "Please, it is a small favor. Let them enter their own father's house and halls."

Oh, thank Zeus!

She watches and listens as Lykos orders his servants to undo the bolts and let the family enter. "I won't begrudge funeral robes." He says as though he is a kind and generous ruler. "Once you are dressed, though, I will consign you to the world below."

After opening the doors to the temple, the king's guards return to their places at his side. He finishes speaking and she watches as they walk off Zeus' soil.

She takes her youngest from her eldest and holds him in her arms. She clasps her hands around the other two. "Come children, follow your poor mother's footsteps into your father's house. Others now own his goods but we still own his name."

The mother and her three children enter Zeus' palace.

Mindless God or No Sense of Justice

Amphitryon stands helplessly and watches his daughter-in-law and grandsons enter Zeus' temple. He hangs his head low in shame. He stands at the base of Zeus' idol, at its feet, and moves his eyes upward until they reach the idol's head.

"What was the point, Zeus?" He mutters. The words come haltingly and painfully. "What was the point of letting you share my wife? What was the point of telling the world that you are my son's half father? I thought you'd turn out to be a better friend than this."

What a pretender. A powerful god without virtue. You are betraying your son's family. I have never betrayed you. You are an expert in betrayal, aren't you? Uninvited, you secretly slid into my wife's bed. You are ignorant about how to act in public. Why won't you save the lives of your dearest friends?

He walks away from Zeus' idol and into his palace. He speaks loudly enough for his old friends to hear. "Zeus, either you are a mindless god or you have no sense of justice."

Heracles Paean (Desire)

The old men huddle together leaning on the sticks. They watch and shake their heads. Powerlessness and shame hang over the old group of former warriors.

The old captain carries a stringed instrument and he steps forward. He places himself at Zeus' feet and faces the group. "I am going to perform as though I were Apollo. He strikes his sweet-tongued lyre with a golden key." He removes a necklace with a spear's metal tip that came close to his heart and plucks a string. "I will do the same for Hercules who has gone under into the gloom of the earth." He begins strumming his lyre and hums. "I want to praise Hercules. Should I call him the son of Zeus or the Amphitryon?" He sees the faces and eyes of his old friends. Note by note, he composes a tune and begins his song.

Hercules, I hope this song I sing in honor of your labors gives you glory for your noble deeds. It is important to praise the work the dead performed. In doing so, we acknowledge their acts of accomplishment. We bring glory to their deeds.

He leads his old battalion in a chant response.

"Hercules, the son of Zeus, rid us of the fierce lion."

"Hercules, the son of Zeus, destroyed the mountain race of wild Centaurs with his arrows."

"Hercules, the son of Zeus, killed a golden horned deer."

The sturdy, heroic, group of brave men are unable to stop tears from flowing down their cheeks. They are not accustomed to womanly tears.

"Hercules, the son of Zeus, killed Diomedes and fed him to his horses."

"Hercules, the son of Zeus, crossed the Hebrus river where he labored for the Mycanaen king."

"Hercules, the son of Zeus, killed Cycnos next to Mount Pelion."

Another old man carries a flute and sits on the ground next to his old comrade. He finds the notes and his sounds join the tune.

"Hercules, the son of Zeus, killed the dragon-guard on Hesperides."

"Hercules, the son of Zeus, saved sailors by calming the waters in the straits of Gadir."

"Hercules, the son of Zeus, helped Atlas hold the heavens."

An old man sits in front of Zeus' temple doors, hits and bangs on a drum, and chants in rhythm with his friends' sounds of honor and fame.

"Hercules, the son of Zeus, fought the Amazons in order to bring their golden girdle to Greece."

"Hercules, the son of Zeus, used fire to kill the Hydra and used its poison to kill Geryon on the island of Erytheia."

The old man with the lyre strums and chords come faster and faster. The flute player blows faster to maintain rhythm. The drummer's steady beat hypnotizes the old men, who have dropped their canes, and forgotten the pains of their old age. "Hercules, the son of Zeus, did all these things and then he sailed to tear-soaked Hades. It was the last labor of his life. He hasn't returned to Thebes and his house is without youthful friends."

The old men, chanting rhythmically, are lost in a trance envisioning their glory days when Thebes was heroic, and the city was free of disease.

"Charon's oar waits to ferry him on a journey down to the underworld. A journey of no return and one which is against the laws of justice - of both the gods and man."

Hercules' old sergeant, leaning on a cane and panting from his hypnotic dance, steps forward. "Hercules, your house - your wife, your three sons, and your father - looks to you, but you are not here to provide protection." He kicks Zeus' soil. "If only I wasn't old and weak. If only I had strength." He places his forehead against the cold marble of Zeus' idol. "If I was young and strong, I could use a war spear. I would stand by your sons, Hercules, if only I was young and strong. But I am old and weak and the city of Thebes is diseased with dissension and civil strife."

Who Will Murder Me?

Cradling her youngest, Megara walks out of the Palace dressed in a funeral robe and wearing a lily wreath of death on her head. Her eldest, also in a robe and lily wreath, follows on his own. They are trailed by Amphytryon, who holds the middle child's hand. They too are dressed in funeral robes and wear lily wreaths of death on their heads.

Magara has transformed herself and holds her chin high. Her inner fear is well-hidden. She has assumed the role of brave Hercules wife.

"Come now and hurry this up. Bring the priest to sacrifice, or butcher, these poor children. We are ready to descend to Hades' halls." She storms around Zeus' temple courtyard. "Who will murder me?"

Where are the executioner's? When will the tyrant king return? We sacrificial victims are ready to be taken to Hades' halls. Look at us. What a pitiful group. A mother, her children, and an old man. An odd

parade of the living dead. A shocking fate for me and

a shocking fate for my children. Oh, my three sons. Let

my eyes fall on you one last time. I gave birth to you yet

I have to watch my enemies insult, torment, and then

kill you. All for their own enjoyment. Hercules had

given me so many words of hope. Those words have

betrayed me.

Megara looks into her eldest son's eyes. "Hercules was going to have you sit on the throne in Argos." She touches his hair. "You were going to wear his great lion skin armor over your head while ruling the great fertile land of the Pelasgians." She walks to her middle child who holds her father-in-law's hand. "Hercules was going to make you the ruler of Thebes - land of chariots. He was going to place a carved wooden club in your right hand to defend against evil." She looks into her infant son's eyes as she cradles him in her arms. "Hercules was going to hand you Oechalia the country he conquered with his far-shooting arrows."

Hercules, my dead husband. You were so proud of your sons' manliness. You had three thrones chosen to exalt each. And I was already choosing the best brides and scheming to make Athens, Thebes, and Sparta allies through marriage. This would have anchored your life's cables and held your sheet-anchor steady.

Attempting to steal herself, she gazes around the temple courtyard. "All that is gone now." She bounces and her infant son's crying body. "The winds of your fortune have veered and turned. Your brides are the spirits of death and they have robbed me of my rights to give you your bridal bath. They only give me tears." She and her father-in-law make eye contact but then quickly look away.

Your grandfather is celebrating your marriage-feast and accepted Hades as the father of your brides.

I don't know which of my sons to press to my bosom, which to kiss first, and which to kiss last. What am I to do? Which should I cling to? I wish I were a bee with golden wings. I'd collect every sigh, blend them together, and shed one copious tear.

She walks to her father-in-law's side and throws her arms over his old shoulders and presses her cheek against his chest. "Please, may your son Hercules hear my mortal words in the halls of Hades. Your father, your sons, and your wife are dying and doomed."

I was once called blessed for marrying you. Come save me. Rescue your family. Even if you only come as a shadow. Your phantom presence would be enough to stop these child-killing cowards.

I Speak in Prayer to Zeus

Amphitryon watches his son's wife. He's proud she's able to hold her chin to the heavens. Her behavior is more honorable and noble than before.

"Megara, daughter-in-law, prepare the funeral rites." He watches her walk to the holy bath and splash water on his grandson's foreheads. He relocates and places himself next to Zeus' idol. He raises his arms to their full length and places his palms against the idol's cold marble stone.

"I raise my hands to the heavens. I speak in prayer to Zeus. I call on you to help your grandchildren." He looks around expectantly. After a moment, he drops his arms, and lowers his head. His voice is barely audible. "Do you intend to help these children? I have prayed and invoked your name my entire life. Will you send aid or be unavailing and force death upon us?" He turns his body toward Zeus' temple and speaks as loudly as he can. "My life's toil has been wasted and my death is inevitable."

He joins his group of old comrades in arms. He grasps their hands and looks into their eyes. "My old and aged friends. Life is too short and the joys of life are few. Live as best you can." He places his arm on his sergeant's shoulder and takes care not to notice the tear welling in his eye. "Take heed and pass through your days and nights as gladly as you may. Be free of sadness and without a thought of sorrow through all time from morning till night." He embraces his sergeant. "Old friends, time does not care about our hopes. He wrecks the little hope." He embraces his captain. "Time flies and passes. Look at me. I am a man who made a mark amongst his fellows and achieved great fame."

He walks to the edge of the cliff and looks down on the city of Thebes. He sighs, groans, and shakes his head. "Among the mortals, I was known for doing great deeds. Fortune in a single day has robbed me of fame. I am like a feather that has been lifted up by wind and floats away toward the sky." He looks at his old friends. They had once been so strong and mighty and they looked so weak and pitiful.

"Wealth, fame, high reputation, none of these are fixed or will stay with you always. Farewell friends of my own age. Look upon your friend for this is the time I shall be seen."

Part II: From Old to New

Do You See a Man?

She watches her father-in-law stand on the cliff's edge looking down on Thebes.

Who is that coming up the hill?

"Father-in-law, do you see a man walking up the hill and toward Zeus' temple? Do I truly behold my dearest husband? I don't know what words to choose or what to say."

Amphitryon stands with his mouth open and eyes wide. "Daughter, I am struck dumb and speechless."

Is this really the man who went beneath the earth? Am I being mocked by a daydream?

Megara starts weeping and the tears stream down her face. "What am I saying? My anxious eyes are not confused. I am not stuck in some dream or vision." She grabs the robes of her two older sons and pushes them toward the temple's entrance.

"Old man, your son has returned. Children, hold and cling onto your father's robe. Hurry and make haste." Watching her two older boys run to their father she looks into her infant's eyes. "Grab your father's robe and never lose your hold. This man will save you as surely as Zeus is the god of this altar."

I Arrived Home to Find Confusion

The group of twenty old men stand in awe as a young man of health and vigor reaches the temple's outer courtyard. He carries a bow in his arm, arrows on his back, and a large club swings on his right side.

"Sons, I'm so happy to find you here." His broad smile reveals his teeth. His eldest and middle son grab onto his garment and press their faces into his legs.

Hercules bends and swoops his middle son into his arms. He places his hand on his eldest son's head and tussles his hair. "Hello to everything and everyone. Hello my home, my doors, my hearth." His legs stride in militant lengths toward his wife. "I feel such joy and gladness to emerge into the light and see you. Ah, what do I see?" Hercules' facial expression changes from supreme gladness to puzzlement.

Why are my sons dressed in funeral garb with lily garlands of death on their heads? Why is this large crowd of old men standing in front of my father's temple? My wife stands deep in a crowd and a throng of men surround my weeping father. None of this is normal. I will draw closer and discover what new stroke of fate has struck my house.

His wife runs toward him. Her eyes are red and crusty, and her nose runs. She throws her body against his and he smells her fearful sweat. "Dearest of all mankind, you've returned into the light and come back to me."

His father walks toward him with outstretched arms.

He holds his body with as much nobility as an old man can muster while leaning on a cane.

"Hercules, my son, you are a ray of light. You have appeared to rescue your father. Is it really you?" He places his palms on Hercules' cheeks and looks into his eyes. "You have arrived just in time."

He accepts his father's kiss on each cheek and returns the gesture. He waves his hand and shakes his head. "Father, I don't understand."

I arrived home to find confusion.

His wife uses her arms to pry his father away from his embrace. "Hercules, my husband, we are ruined. We are about to be killed." She looks at her father-in-law, asks him to lean down, and she speaks into his ear. "Forgive me if I snatched words out of your mouth. You have more right to say the words than I." She places her lips against his cheeks and then walks toward her husband's embrace. "It is a woman's nature to speak in anguish and my children and I were being led to death."

Oh, Apollo! What a sad prelude to your story.

His wife leans her head against his muscular chest covering his beating heart. She speaks into his flesh. "Hercules, my brothers and father Creon are all dead."

"What happened? Who killed them?" He grabs her shoulders and gives her a shake.

His wife's eyes well with tears and she begins weeping. "Our new monarch, the tyrant Lykos, killed them."

Hercules looks at his father. "How did these deaths take place? Was it in a fair fight or battle?" Hercules walks to the edge of the cliff and looks down on the city of Thebes. He had heard rumors. He speaks into the wind. "When king Creon was murdered, was the country suffering from affliction?

Was the land sick and weak? Was the city rife with dissension and civil strife?"

His wife comes from behind and places her palm on his shoulder. "Yes, husband, Thebes is sick with faction and civil war." He turns to face her and she throws herself against his brawny chest. "Now the tyrant king rules and is master of Cadmus' city of seven gates."

He holds his wife and presses her tightly against his body. "When I arrived, why were you terrified and panicked?"

His wife weeps uncontrollable into his chest. "The tyrant king was going to kill your father, me, and our sons.

Deserted by Everyone

Megara holds onto her husband, her cheeks pressed against his strong chest, and her arms stretched across his broad back. She explained the funeral robes and lly wreaths of death. She couldn't finish without weeping uncontrollably.

Hercules' words address the top of her head. "He feared my orphan babies?"

Her cheeks are pressed against his chest. "He was afraid they would avenge Creon's death."

"My sons are dressed as though they're heading to their own funeral."

She inhales his odor and presses her cheek harder onto his chest. "Your children wear the garbs of death for their funeral."

His body rocks with her's in disbelief. "This tyrant king was going to kill all of you and you were going to die a violent, terrible death." She feels his warm breath on her scalp.

"Hercules, my husband, we have been deserted by every friend. Everyone spoke the words and said you were dead."

His heart races against her cheek. "And you were desperate and accepted their words as true? Speak the name. Who put such a bleak thought in your heads?"

"Eurystheus' heralds and messengers proclaimed this as true."

He breathes onto her scalp and holds her for a moment. Then he breaks her grasp, lifts her chin, and looks her in the eyes. "Why do you abandon my home and hearth?"

"We were forced." She points toward her father-in-law. "They even tossed and dragged your father from his bed."

Her husband's face turns crimson red and his body tenses with rage. "The tyrant king and the young men of Thebes have no mercy or shame? They treat an old man so poorly?"

"Mercy or shame?" She spits the words with a rueful laugh. "Lykos doesn't know the goddess."

Hercules looks at the group of old men and then at his wife. "Was I so poor in friends? Were they rare in my absence?"

Again, she spits the words with a rueful laugh. "Who has friends during a time of misfortune?"

"They make light of, and forget, my warring with the Minyae?"

She smiles, then weeps, then presses her cheek against her husband's chest. "Husband, I'll speak the words again. Misfortune has no friends."

What Was the Point of my Labors?

Hercules drops his hands from his wife's shoulders. He repeatedly balls his big, meaty hands and then opens hands to spread his fingers wide. His face is aflame, his eyes flash, and his words are like fire.

He uses his regimental commander's voice. "All of you, right now. Remove these lily wreaths of death from your heads." He grabs his middle and eldest sons under their arms. "Look up to the light and behold the welcome sun. Forget the underworld's nether gloom. As for me, my hands will work."

I shall tear down the upstart king's palace, cut off the shameless heads of all conspiring Thebans, and throw them to the dogs to gnaw at. I shall seek out Thebans who thought little of me and played the traitor. I will give them a taste of my glorious club. The rest will become mangled corpses in the river Ismenus. Once my flying arrows reach their bodies, my feathered shafts will turn the Spring of Dirce red with their bloody corpses.

He turns and addresses the group of twenty old men. "If I don't defend my wife, my children, and my old father then who should I defend? What was the point of my labors?" He walks towards Zeus' temple and looks up at Zeus' face. "I should have stayed here to defend my boys. They were about to die for their father.   Was it more virtuous a deedt to obey Eurystheus and kill the hydra than protecting my children from slaughter?"

If I can't defend my own family why should I be thought of as virtuous? What good are the words, 'Hercules the Victor,' if I have no virtue?

Don't be Hasty

Amphitryon puffs his chest when he hears his old sergeant. "The words Hercules chooses are proper. Fathers should help their children, their own fathers, and their wives."

Proud of his son's words he lifts his eyes to heaven, holds them there for a moment of reflection, and then faces his son. "My son, your nature is to love your friends and hate your enemies." He places his hand on his son's lower back - it's all he can reach - with the intent of providing a warm, loving touch. "But don't be hasty."

His son flinches. "How could I be too hasty?"

I was afraid of this. My son isn't aware of how many allies and friends this tyrant king has collected. It would take too long to explain the political complexities. Thebes suffers too much dissension and civil strife. Poor people boast of wealth and a group has banded together to conspire. Intent on sowing dissension they want to break the city and plunder their neighbors' wealth. It will take too long to explain how these villains lost their own wealth through laziness and sloth.

"My son, you were seen entering the city. I don't want your enemies to come together and slay you unawares."

I Saw This Omen

His son walks to the bench where he placed his bow, grabs it, and holds it in his right hand. "Father, I don't care if everyone in the city saw me." Standing erect and proud, his son looks at Zeus' idol.

"However, by chance, just before I entered the city, I saw a bird perched on an ill-omened branch. From the bird's position, I realized trouble had befallen my house. Because I saw this omen, I took heed and entered with stealth.

Reminded me of Telemachus

As he was speaking a bird flew by upon his right hand--a hawk, Apollo's messenger. It held a dove in its talons, and the feathers, as it tore them off, {138} fell to the ground midway between Telemachus and the ship. On this Theoclymenus called him apart and caught him by the hand. "Telemachus," said he, "that bird did not fly on your right hand without having been sent there by some god. As soon as I saw it I knew it was an omen; it means that you will remain powerful and that there will be no house in Ithaca more royal than your own." "I wish it may prove so," answered Telemachus. "If it does, I will show you so much good will and give you so many presents that all who meet you will congratulate you." Then he said to his friend Piraeus, "Piraeus, son of Clytius, you have throughout shown yourself the most willing to serve me of all those who have accompanied me to Pylos; I wish you would take this stranger to your own house and entertain him hospitably till I can come for him."

Do Not Act

Praise Zeus. Thank you for providing our son with a lucky omen.

"My son, go inside your father's temple and give thanks. Salute the goddess of your altar. Let your father's face see your face."

He is too great a warrior but I hope he moves quickly. The tyrant king is going to return in person to drag us away and slaughter your babies, your wife, and add your old father to the bloody list.

"My son, please stay up here with your family and your father Zeus. We will profit from this security. Do not go into the city and get it all stirred up." He looks at the group of twenty old men. "My son, do not act until you have everything well prepared."

His son holds the bow and paces a bit. His face is flush with anger and every muscle in his body is tense. After a few minutes of pacing, the color in his face subsides. "Father, your advice is good and I shall do as you say. I am going to step inside and enter my father's house." His son faces and speaks to the twenty old warriors. "I have come back up here after returning from the sunless den of Hades. After meeting the maiden queen of hell, I will not neglect the respect and greetings due the gods beneath my roof."

He beams with pride. "You went down into the house of Hades?"

"Yes father, I did. And I brought Cerberus, the three-headed beast, up to the light of the sun.

He shakes his head in awe. "Did you fight or did the goddess present it to you?"

His son smiles a noble smile. "It was a fair fight. I was blessed, I had the good fortune, to have witnessed the Eleusinian mysteries before I descended into Hades."

"So, the beast is in the halls of Eurystheus?"

His son stands tall and speaks so all his old comrades can hear. "I have imprisoned Cerebaus Detemer's grove inside the city of Hermione."

He smiles at his twenty old friends. His son's words and deeds help him stand strong. "Does Eurystheus know you've returned to the world of the light?"

"No, not yet. I've made my way here first to see how things were with you."

A Youthful and Strong Friend

Hercules works to maintain his composure but inside he is a raging storm. He has acquiesced to his father's request only because he fears for his family's safety.

If only I had youthful and strong friends right here on Zeus' soil. I would leave my family under their protection and go into Thebes to kill this tyrant king.

His father is speaking. "What?"

"I said, what kept you in the underworld for so long?"

He smiles at the thought of the name. "Theseus. He was down in the underworld below. I had to bring him back up here into the light."

"Where is Theseus? In his homeland?"

"Yes, he returned to Athens." He laughs as he remembers their parting. "The poor man was glad to have escaped from the lower world."

Big Ship that Tugs Little Boats

Right!

He looks at his two older sons and then at his infant in his wife's arms. "Boys, wife, all of you come with me and let's enter into my father's house together." He scratches his son's head. "Going into the temple like this together is better than coming out in death robes, right boys?"

His sons didn't appreciate the joke. Their effort at manhood has disappeared. "Have courage, boys. My sons, dry the tears from your eyes." He lifts his eyes to look at his wife and sees her weeping in fear. "Dear wife, gather your courage and cease your fear." He pries at his sons' grasping fingers. "Boys, let go of your father's robe. I'm no feathered bird that is going to fly away from the ones I love."

The children do not loosen their hold, but cling to my garments more strongly. They're pulling harder.

Was there such jeopardy?   Were their lives in such danger? From this moment forward, I will lead them by the hand.   To draw their foes after me, I will act like the big ship towing their little boats.   From now on, I'll be in front and I'll tow all of them safely inside the harbor behind me.

He turns toward the group of twenty old men and looks each in the eye. He speaks clearly. "I won't neglect the care of my children. Mankind is equal in this regard. Rich or poor, the entire human race loves their own children."

Hercules Paean (Celebration)

The twenty old men are dispersed throughout the courtyard. Celebratory notes, sounds, and songs dance in the air. The old men rhythmically throw their bodies to lyre, flute, and drum. In response to Hercules return, the old men ecstatically praise the gods.

"I love youth." One of the old men places his cane on Zeus' soil and sways in the tune-filled air.

"Old age is a burden heavier than the boulders on Mt Aetna. It casts a pall of gloom all over my head and upon my eyes." Another old man is rocking his body back and forth, nodding his head to the drummer's beat.

"Give me youth!" The old sergeant, twirling, has found himself on the cliff's edge looking down on the city of Thebes below. He shouts at the citizens in the marketplace underneath Zeus' temple. "You can keep all the wealth of Asia's kings and all the houses full of gold."

"Youth, gasp, is better, gasp, when in wealth, gasp, or poverty." The old captain wheezes and he grasps his heart. He suffers from old age and too much dithyrambic celebration.

"Old age is a, wheeze, gloomy and deathly, wheeze, thing." The sergeant has walked away from the cliff's edge. He gasps for breath and sits on a bench.

All the music has stopped. The old men are in different positions of repose attempting to regain their strength. In their celebration to Zeus for Hercules' return, they forgot who they were. They are the old men of Thebes. They no longer possess health, youth, or vigor. They represent all the disease, dissension, and civil strife in the city of Thebes. They reveal the truth about Thebans, the city lacks healthy, honorable, and noble warrior men.

"I hate old age." One of the old men sits on Zeus' soil with his lyre on the ground by his side. "Let it sink and vanish beneath the ocean's waves!"

"I wish old age would never have found its way into mortal homes and cities." An old warrior, whose friends thought stronger, surrenders to the goddess Algea and womanly tears flow from his eyes down his cheeks. His tearing eyes look at the face of Zeus' idol.

"It should have stayed up drifting through the upper air's winds."

Having regained his breath, one of the old men struggles to his feet. He balances himself on his cane and walks to the cliff's edge and looks down on the city of Thebes. "If the gods truly had wisdom, and could discern the true reasons for the actions of mortals, they'd grant virtuous mortals youth twice." Old men wholeheartedly speak words of agreement with a chorus of 'Hear! Hear!' He hears their words and continues. "After death, the gods would reward the virtuous and the moral would receive a visible mark. After entering Hades, the underworld below, this visible mark of virtue and worth would allow the mortal to retrace their steps once more to the sun-light." The old man looks at his old comrades in arms. Warriors with whom he fought many battles and helped Alphitryon bring health and civic virtue to Thebes. "The virtuous mortal could start their life again and the mean man would have only one single life." 'Hear! Hear!' "Men could then distinguish themselves and find the virtuous just as sailors discern the number of stars through clouds. As things stand, the gods have provided no means to distinguish the good and the bad."

An old man stands next to him and also looks down on the citizens in the city of Thebes below. "Time's onward roll only brings increase to man's wealth."

An old man sits on a bench in Zeus' and tightens his lyre's. He has not yet spoken. He has only listened as his old warrior friends speak about old age. He begins to pluck chords. "The Graces and the Muses are the sweetest union. The two shall always be one in my mind." He glances to his right. He sees his best friend, the man he relied on in battle, and his heart relives the wars. Two men standing next to one another, back to back, with spears and shields. And nothing between life in light and death in the darkness below, except fate, trust in the gods, and mortal hope. "I hope I'll never be without songs but always placed in the choir. I am an old singer and so I shall lift up my voice and sing to praise Mnemosyne, the mother of bygone memories."

His friend smiles. Memories of their warrior days fill his heart with happiness and joy. He places his flute in front of his lips. "Whether I am drunk on Bacchus' wine, or accompanied by the seven-stringed lyre and the Libyan flute, I sing to praise Hercules' glorious victories."

The group of twenty old men of Thebes began by celebrating Hercules' return and then felt their old age. Now, their lyre- and flute-playing comrades have reminded them of Hercules' return from the underworld below.

Leaning against his cane, an old man faces Zeus' temple. "My aged lips, brought to the dance by the song of joy from maids of Delos I love, will sing songs of victory and glory while I dance gracefully around your palace doors."

An old man stands near a dear old friend so he may feel the warmth of his body. "A minstrel song of my old age. In honor of Apollo I will sing, like an aged swan about to die, around the temple's gates."

An old man embraces another and they look down on Thebans in the city below. "What a theme to sing about. Hercules, born by Zeus high above his noble birth tower, and his toil secured this life of calm for man."

"Hercules destroyed all the fearsome and gruesome beasts."

Die on the Conditions You Offered

King Lykos stands on Zeus' soil, inside the courtyard, and in front of Zeus' temple. He glances at the group of old men standing around his guards. The old man walks out of the temple in a funeral robe but he doesn't wear a lily wreath of death on his head. "About time you came out of that palace, Amphitryon. Your putting on and arraying yourselves in funeral clothes has taken up too much time. Enough with the robes and trappings of the dead." He claps his hand. "Come now, do as you've promised. Speak and tell Hercules' wife and sons to show themselves outside. Tell them to come out here and prepare to die on the conditions you yourselves offered."

Truly! I need to get back to the master of coin. I have devised a new scheme for dissension and civil strife.

The old man wears a pathetic expression on his face. "My king. Why do you persecute me for my misery? Your zeal is over and above the loss of my son, sir. You should be more moderate." The old man bends to one knee and lowers his head.

That's a good show of respect. Much better than before.

"You are my lord and master but, lord or not, I ask that you temper your zeal. Stop your insults while I grieve." He rises. "But, yes, since you impose and press us to death's stern necessity, we acquiesce. We are ready to do your will."

Excellent.

The king looks around the courtyard. "Where is Megara? Where are the sons of Hercules?"

Where are Alcmene's grandchildren?

The old man looks to his left, then to his right, then he turns around. He shrugs his shoulders and points to a gate at the entrance to Zeus' temple. "I believe, I guess, so far as I can make out, from outside, looking through this gate..."

Speak!

The king walks toward the gate and prepares to peer inside Zeus' temple. "What is she doing? What's going on? What do you see?"

Provide reasons not fancy, old man.

Resurrect Him

He looks at the tyrant king and sees a man with no nobility or honor. A man who happily and lasciviously looks forward to roasting his grandsons alive. He doesn't see a man.

"My king, looking inside Zeus' temple, I see her sitting as a supplicant on the hallowed steps of Hestia's altar."

He feels the king's frustration in his words. "Obviously. Praying uselessly and imploring to save her life."

This man has no respect for the gods! Doesn't he know whom he speaks to? Zeus cuckolded my wife and gave birth to my son, Hercules, who brought health, vitality, and peace to Thebes.

He bows his head. "Yes, that's right my king, she's praying in vain. She's calling her dead husband back to life."

The tyrant king throws his back and laughs. His white teeth are visible in his foreign black face. "A husband who is nowhere near, nowhere seen, or will ever be seen. He is a husband who will never return."

Good. Word of my son's return has not yet reached his ears. His eyes are still in the dark.

"Unless, perhaps, a god should resurrect him and raise him from the dead?"

The tyrant king doesn't give the thought a moment's reflection. The king turns to his guards, points at Amphitryon, and barks. "Go to her inside the palace and bring her out here..

The guards each place hands on his biceps and drag him toward the temple. "If I do as you ask, and bring my daughter-in-law and grandsons outside, I'll be complicit in her murder." The guards continue to drag him toward the temple's gate. "My king, will you make me an accomplice?"

The tyrant king motions with his hand and lifts his chin. The guards let go of Amphitryon's biceps. "Such a scruple." He smiles, chuckles, and shakes his head. "If this bothers you, I will bring them out myself." The tyrant king turns and faces his old warrior friends. "I have left fear behind and will bring out the mother and her children. Follow me, servants, no more delay. Time for our work of joy." Smiling and laughing, the tyrant king walks into Zeus' temple. "Time to put a painless ending to this troublesome affair."

He watches the tyrant king and his guards enter the temple. He turns his head to look at his old warrior friends. His face transforms as he smiles happily.

Walk along the path. Go meet your fate. You perform evil deeds and others pay the price.

He walks toward the group of twenty old friends and huddles with his old sergeant and captain. "Old and aged friends, the tyrant Lykos enters the temple at precisely the right time. This murderer marches fairly to his doom. He hopes to kill but will soon be entangled in a snare." He places his arm on his sergeant's shoulder and both their faces shine bright with pleasure. "Hercules' sword is waiting for him inside Zeus' temple. This villain thinks he will slay his neighbors." He separates himself and walks toward Zeus' gate and prepares to enter the temple. "I am going inside the temple to watch the tyrant king fall and die."

The sight of a foe, an evil enemy, being slain provides pleasure. Watching an enemy pay the full price for his deeds provides good feelings.

Part III: From Wolf to Wolfish Rage

Thebes' Paean (Revenge)

Inside the courtyard, directly outside the gate of Zeus' temple, the twenty old men huddle. Old men play lyres, flutes, and drums. No one dances as the sounds of the music remain low in the background.

Evil has changed sides and fortunes have turned.

The sounds of instruments filling the air, some old men relocate, and position themselves so they can touch the cold, smooth marble of Zeus' idol.

Our once great mighty king has returned backward from the road to Hades.

Hercules is alive! Hail justice and heavenly retribution.

The ever-turning will of the gods floods down.

Without entering Zeus' temple, the old captain steps forward and attempts to peer within. He turns toward his comrades-in-arms. "This tyrant enters the palace of his death. He will be punished by death for the insolence shown against his betters. Joy floods my eyes and makes tears burst forth."

Hercules, the true king of this land, has returned. A thing never once thought in my heart.

Retribution has been beyond my hopes and expectations.

The old men group together directly outside the gate to Zeus' temple where they can only see a foyer marble entrance. "Come, old friends. Let's look inside the palace. I hope we see one we know meet the fate he deserves."

From inside the temple they hear screaming sounds. At first, the sounds are faint and faroff. Then they become louder and they hear echoes of the tyrant king's hysterical voice.

"Help me!"

The tyrant king screams like a woman.

The old captain turns to his old sergeant, lifts his chin, and smiles broadly. "Within the house, I hear the song's sweet opening note of his doom. Death is not far off him."

The tyrant king's voice can be heard clearly in Zeus' courtyard. His screams rise and fall in volume as he runs throughout the temple's rooms.

"Help me!"

Not long now!

Listen to the sweet groans.

Glorious cries of agony that prelude a tyrant's death.

The tyrant king's voice is no longer hysterically screaming or changing in sound. Outside in the courtyard, in front of Zeus' temple, the group of old men hear the tyrant's dying words.

"Treachery! Thebans, help me. Sons of Cadmus, come to my rescue." The tyrant's voice is barely a whisper. "I'm being murdered. Treachery!"

An old lyre player plucks, a flute player blows, and a drummer bangs. Old men speak over one another and sway to music.

"Yes!"

"Treachery for treachery, Ly..."

"Prepare yourself for retributi..."

"Lykos, you weak mortal, you aimed impious and blasphem..."

"You maintained the gods are nothing but weaklings. Such a stupid thin..."

The captain presses his body against the gate and listens. He turns toward the group of twenty old men and sees they are playing music, laughing, and speaking words of merriment. "Old friends, listen with your ears. Not a sound. Our godless foe is no more." The old captain lifts his walking cane. He holds it as though it were a spear and was back in his youthful days of vigor and health. "The palace is still.

Let us begin our dancing and rejoicing. The blasphemer is no more!"

A group of old men stand at the cliff's edge and look down on the city of Thebes below. One of them shouts so the citizens can hear. "The holy city of Thebes shall celebrate with dances and banquets. Changed paths have released us from tears. Fortune from sorrow now gives birth to new songs." He laughs and embraces an old warrior.

"The upstart king is dead and gone. Our former monarch has risen and the tyrant is left on the banks of Acheron."

Hope beyond hope has happened.

The gods take note of evil and good.

Right and wrong is in heaven's care.

Two old men stand at the base of Zeus' idol. They place their palms and foreheads against the cold marble. Their call and response words are in time with the musical notes.

"When men's hearts acquire gold."

"Good fortune drags."

"Minds away from logic."

"Toward unjust power."

The twenty old men have forgotten all emotional restraint. Old, proud warriors whose eyes never before shed tears, weep openly. Sounds of praise and joy fill the air.

Two sober and serious old men stand at the cliff's edge looking down on the city of Thebes below. "While committing crimes and rejoicing in their disdain for the law, men lack the courage of reflection. They cannot imagine how time can reverse fortunes."

"Yes, fortune can always shatter and smash wealth's dark chariot."

In a part of the courtyard near a bench, a group of old men stand and sit. A lyre player plugs his chords and they nod their heads listening to his choral words. "Sing, river Ismenos and deck your heads with garlands. Dance, city of Thebes and may your paved streets break forth."

Another old lyre player joins their group and plucks his chords. "River Dirce, you of the lovely waters, and daughters of Asopos, leave your father's waters and waves. Add your maiden voices to our hymn. Sing with me this victory prize that Hercules has won."

A third old man joins with his voice as his only instrument. "You too, Parnassus, with your crowned woods and forests, Apollo's holy cliff, and the Muses on Helicon. Add to our voices of joy. Crowd out my city and my city's walls."

A group of old men engage in a chant and call response.

"Make my city and her walls re-echo with cries of joy."

"A generation of men have sprung forth from the earth in this city."

"Warriors with shields of bronze and brass."

"Thebes is a sacred and divine light passed and handed to children's children."

A group of old men stand by the base of Zeus' idol and pass amphoras of wine. They make toasts, salute one another, and salute the gods. The wine and the joy have helped them regain the healthy vigor of youth.

"Hail the cuckolded marriage." The group of men shout 'Hear! Hear!'

"Two bridegrooms, Amphitryon and Zeus, shared Alcmene's bed."

"An ancient tale, once hard to believe, has been proved a true story."

An old man pours amphora directly into his mouth. When he finishes red liquid flows down his chin. "Zeus has made clear Hercules' power. It is a hope beyond all hope that Hercules arrived to provide mortal man with protection."

"Yes, time has shown Hercules' might and the luster of his prowess."

An old man has finished embracing another and reaches for an amphora. He's shaking his head in disbelief. "For his most recent labor, bright Hercules sprung up from the caverns of the earth below."

"Hercules," every amphora in the courtyard is raised, "you are a worthier king than that crass tyrant."

"This struggle between armed warriors will decide Lykos' fate."

"We will see if the gods in heaven still love justice and the just deed."

Don't Sleep with my Husband

Hercules' father, the god Zeus, lives and sits on a throne within Olympus, high in the heavens above the city of Thebes. Zeus has a wife, the goddess Hera, and she sits by his side. Hera has despised Hercules since the moment Zeus disguised himself and impregnated Alcmene with Hercules. From before his birth, while he was still emerging within the womb, Hera focused on making Hercules suffer.

Hera is repaying the half-mortal for his mortal mother's adulterous betrayal with her husband. When the mortal woman tried to appease Hera by naming the half-mortal "glorious gift of Hera," she was not amused. Her anger increased as she watched Hercules grow and saw his fame spread.

Hera has a handmaid goddess whose name is Iris. Iris is a beautiful virgin with golden wings. She carries a herald's staff in one arm and a vase in the other. A rainbow surrounds her buzzing wings. Born of the sea-god Thaumas and the cloud-nymph Elektra, Iris is Hera's personal messenger.

Iris descends from the heavens and appears above the twenty old men dispersed throughout the courtyard. They continue playing music, drinking, and celebrating Hercules' return.

The goddess Lyssa appears next to Iris. Lyssa, daughter of primordial Titans, linked by blood to the night, and relative to the spirits, Maniae, wears nothing but a short skirt and a dog's head. The two goddesses hover in the air above Zeus' temple and watch the mortals celebrate. They become angry when their presence isn't noticed and they descend rapidly with a thud on the temple's roof.

Wolfish Rage

Well, that got the mortals' attention. Look at them scurry about.

Below the temple, on Zeus' soil, the twenty old men have stopped their celebrations and their hands have dropped their musical instruments. Lyssa is amused.

Old men scurry and run in Zeus' courtyard. They knock one another over and their old age prevents them from rising. Those who can fall on their knees and face Zeus. The goddess smiles.

"Old friends!" Lyssa listens to the mortal's words. "An ominous apparition has descended and hovers over the palace. Run, run away friends."

Look at their fear and panic.

"Run!"

"Rush your tardy feet and run!"

"Lord Apollo! Lord, save us from this terror!"

Where do they think they're going to run and hide? We are goddesses! Stupid mortals..

Iris speaks. "Have courage, men. Don't be afraid." The messenger uses her wings to fly and hover above the old men. "I am Iris, handmaiden of the gods, and this is Madness, daughter of Night. We have not come to harm you or your city. We are marshaling for war against the house of one single man - Hercules, the son of Zeus and Alcmene."

The old men don't know what to do.

Iris points at Zeus' temple. "Now that Hercules' has accomplished his labors, neither fate nor Zeus can protect him from Hera's harm. Hera wants to stain him with the guilt of shedding kindred blood." She uses her wings and flies to the roof of Zeus' temple. She speaks to the group of twenty old men and delivers Hera's message. "Hercules will slay his own children and wear the brand of spilling his sons' blood." She turns and faces Lyssa. "And I agree with her on this decision."

Iris is focused on punishing Hercules. I think she approves of this decision a bit too much. This shouldn't be such a pleasant task.

Iris is imploring Lyssa to follow Hera's command. "Come, unmarried virgin, daughter of black Night, harden your ruthless heart. Be relentless." She leans in close and breathes the words onto Lyssa's skin. "Send your child-murdering frenzy forth upon Hercules. Stir up and confound his mind. Make his feet twitch and shudder."

Hera demands I goad Hercules, wind him up, and shake out his sails of death.

Iris' mouth foams. "His own murderous hand will send his precious sons to Acheron's ferry in the world below. He will kill his children and then he will understand fiercely against him the raging anger Hera burns against him." She uses her wings and flies high in the heavens above Zeus' temple and looks down. Her words carry in the sky and reach down into the city of Thebes below. "If this man escapes punishment, the gods will become nothing and the mortals' power will become everything."

Spare Hera and I Your Advice

These are the moments she lives for. Sure, bringing the rainbows is nice. It's pleasant being a beautiful bridge between the sea and sky but also so boring. But, to be a part of murdering a half-mortal? How often does that happen? This act is something to be proud of. All those goddesses, nymphs, and muses back in Olympus who have demeaned her and said she is nothing more than a messenger. Fate has provided her this opportunity. She will show them. She will have the last laugh. When Hera's deeds are remembered, people will speak of Hercules' punishment. Her name will survive the eons. Where will they be?

Lyssa calls and requests she fly closer to the roof of Zeus' temple. She obliges and listens. "Iris, my father, Night, sprung from Titan Ouranos' blood. This noble birth grants me honors and prerogatives."

What is she saying?

"I don't get any joy out of visiting the homes of men, and I don't use my power in anger against friends. Before I begin, Iris, I wish to counsel Hera and offer some advice before a grave error is made. If you will accept them, please hear my words."

Aagghh! I can't interrupt a goddess while she delivers a speech but she is wasting time. I have delivered Hera's message.

Lyssa speaks in a patronizing tone. "Both gods and mortals hold Hercules in high regard. He tamed the impassable land and the wild seas. On his own, with his mighty hand, he restored honor to the gods when godless men were destroying it with impiety."

Does Lyssa understand that this is a direct message from Hera?

Lyssa sees inside Iris' eyes. "My personal counsel, I would rather be his friend than his enemy.

I advise you not to plot evil against him. Do not wish him dire mishaps."

This is really too much!

"Lyssa, spare both Hera and I your advice. It is not needed."

"I am trying to turn your steps." Lyssa's tone has become humiliating. "I want you to see the right way, not the wrong way. The best path instead of one of evil."

Does she think she is better than me? Better than Hera?

"Lyssa, Zeus' wife did not send you here to talk of self-control or wisdom."

Hunting Hound Following a Hunter

Zeus, I tried.

Lussa nods her head at Iris, adjusts her dog's head, and straightens her skirt. She motions for all the old men in the courtyard to come forward. They step forward fearfully, their bodies trembling and liquid seeping through their skins. "I call Apollo the sun-god as my witness. The act I am about to perform is an act I perform against my will. I shall perform and serve Hera's wishes." The soles of her feet are planted on the roof of Heracles' house.

Μένος

Ménos

Mind

Derived from men-

"To think"

She raises her arms and tilts her chin toward the sky. A southerly wind begins to blow. "I follow you as a hunting hound follows a hunter." The dog's head Lussa wears transforms itself. No longer a covering, the dog's head has replaced her own. She barks her words, as she growls and snaps at the old men.

"I am forced headlong into Hercules' breast." Her body, which had before been dense and stable, transforms into an apparition that dives head forward through and into Hercules' roof. Her dive ends when the old men are only able to see the lower half of her torso. The old warriors, who had all been brave hoplite fighters, shake in fear watching Lussa's legs kick in the air. Though her dog's head speaks inside Hercules' house and home, her words reach the ears of all twenty old men.

"The ocean's moaning and groaning waves, the earth's quaking, the pain of the thunderbolt blasting the air. None will be as furious as my rush into Hercules' breast."

Where is that half-mortal? My hunt will end soon.

"I shall crash and burst my way through the roof of his house." Lussa's dog's head apparition is fully within Hercules' home. "I will go through all the rooms of his house." Saliva from her dog's head drips

99

throughout every room. "I will kill his children first. The murderer himself will not know that he is killing his own sons until I have released him from my madness."

Μανία

Maníā

Madness

Derived from μαίνομαι

Maínomai

"I am mad"

Lussa summons the Night and the inside of Hercules' home becomes black. Her southerly winds whip into Hercules' home and shift from strong to gentle. This shift in wind melts and diffuses the condensed air contained within the veins of Hercules' brain.

Lussa understands that the brain, through air, exercises the greatest power in man. When air enters the body properly, the brain is in a sound state. Air supplies sense to the eyes, the ears, the tongue, and the feet. The brain is able to cogitate in as much as it is supplied with air. Air imparts sense to the body.

Lussa enters Hercules' breast to travel the blood vessels into the brain. The brain is the messenger to understanding. When the man draws breath into himself it passes first to the brain and the air is distributed to the rest of the body. The best air, the acme, remains in the brain. Sense and understanding are provided by air, therefore it must go to the brain first. If the air had first passed to the body and then to the brain, it would have left in the flesh and veins judgment. By the time it reached the brain, the air would be mixed with hot blood, humid, and not at all pure.

Lussa's wind has humidified the air inside the veins inside Hercules' brain. This process of air dissolving, condensing, and humidifying is the same process that takes place on the land, the sea, the fountains, and in the wells. Hercules' brain feels the effects of this wind, and his clear thoughts become cloudy. The air in his brain shifts from hot to cold and from dry to moist.

Outside Hercules' home, she increases the southerly wind and the gale's force causes the men to fall down.

κύνα λυσσητῆρα

Lyssētēr kuōn

Martial fury

Rabid dog

Lussa reappears in solid form and stands on the roof of Hercules' home. The roof has been transformed so that it is now transparent and the twenty old men can see inside. She tilts her head to look at a wide-smiling, beaming Iris whose wings allow her to hover in place.

I think she is too happy about delivering a message that will birth within the mortals a new way of thinking.

Lussa looks over the group of twenty old men and points down into the transparent roof under her feet. "Look and behold! Do you see Hercules?" Her dog's head has transformed itself back into its original covering and her beautiful face speaks the words. "He wildly tosses his head without a word out of his mouth. He rolls his frenzied eyes from side to side." Her eyes are locked on Iris'. "He can't control his breath. He pants like a bull preparing to charge. Hear his fearful bellows!" The outside air fills with a blood-curdling scream. "Look and listen! Hercules calls on the nether hell death spirits of Tartarus."

Yes! Call on the monsters within the deep abyss. Reach down into the dungeon of torment and suffering. Bring them all up into the light. Bring them to life!

Lussa's dog's head transforms itself again and attaches to her body. Her body becomes immaterial and she descends partway through the roof to Hercules' home. "Ah, Hercules! Soon I will have roused you to even wilder dancing. I will have your ears hear the notes from the flute of terror." She is about to complete her feet-first descent through Hercules' roof, her neck and head are all that remain. Before entering into his home, she locks eyes with Iris. "Fly away, Iris. Pick up your noble feet and return to Olympus. I will walk unseen into the halls of Hercules' palace."

Lussa hears Iris' laughter and imagines her flying through the heavens shouting the message so Hera   can   hear.

Lament, O City

The twenty old men are in abject terror and despair. They run around the courtyard in all directions. They have all lost their way.

"Lament, O City." An old man screams at the edge of the cliff.

An old man runs to stand next to him and, in a womanly display not worthy of the old warriors, breaks into despair. "Thebans cry!"

The two men look at one another and speak in unison. "Groan and sigh."

Two old men stand at Zeus' altar. "Hercules, son of Zeus, your fairest bloom is being cut down."

"The city is about to lose its flower - Zeus' son!"

An old man lifts his fist into the sky and screams into the heavens. "Greece, you are doomed!"

An old man, who had danced with the lyre and led others in song, weeps while sitting on a bench. "You are casting off and losing your great benefactor."

One of the old men has climbed onto the hill overlooking Hercules' home and attempts to look through Heracles' roof, which Lussa has left transparent. He offers a report to the other old men, who crain their necks and place cupped hands next to their ears.

"He is being destroyed with wild dance. He is dancing to the frenzied sounds of a flute - where no pipe is heard." The old man, holding onto the hill by a sturdy vine, almost loses his balance. He regains control and continues with his report. "Lussa, the Gorgon of the Night and the goddess of sorrow and sighing, has already mounted her chariot. She prods her horses to destruction." He is shouting at the group of old men below and they hear the sorrow in his voice. A group of fierce warrior men are weeping like maidens. "One hundred hissing serpent-heads flashing madness in the eyes. How quickly fate has turned against the fortunate!" The old man climbs down and stands next to his old comrades-in-arms. "Soon the sons will breathe their last. The sons will be murdered by their father's hand vengeance, mad, relentless...."

The old man stops as the group hears their old friend Amphitryon screaming from within Hercules' home. "Ah, misery!"

The twenty old men avoid looking at one another, kick the soil at their feet, and lower their heads in shame. "Zeus, soon your only son will be destroyed through mad and relentless spirits of vengeance. This is an unjust punishment and a cruel death."

The old men hear their old friend scream again. "Ah, roofs of my poor house!"

Ashamed of themselves, not wanting physical contact, they relocate and stand apart in the courtyard.

Sounds from the bowels of Hades emerge from inside Hercules' home. The old sergeant looks at the old captain. "The dance begins without a drum, a cymbal's crash or a waving of Dionysius' staff."

Run, children! Run!

The southerly wind blows Amphitryon throughout Hercules' house in darkness. He has lost his senses. His hands are no longer able to feel the walls and the soles of his feet do not feel firm on the floor. "Ah, the halls of my house!"

Running in blackness, Amphitryon's body diaphragm pulsates. Blood circulates in the wrong direction. His innards are full of bilious air. He has entered into a state of frenzied fear. His old warrior's breath, that kept him alive and heroic on the hoplite battlelines, has deserted him. The humidity in his brain seeps into the ventricles feeding his ears. Within the house of Hercule's there is the pitch blackness of sight of sound.

The only sounds he hears come from outside. He hears the faint words of his old warrior friends, men who stood with him on Hoplite lines fighting alongside one another, backs leaning against backs.

His old friends speak. "The dance in these halls ends in bloodshed. Libations will be poured from spilled blood, not wine."

What has happened to my son, Heracles, born of Zeus? Why is this tragedy befalling me? What is happening to my grandsons? Is Zeus forsaking me? Why have I been so proud of his bedding my wife? Why would Zeus treat me this way? My entire life, I have done nothing except worship and praise his name. Why does he forsake me?

The humidifying process inside the blood vessels inside his brain contracts his lungs. He can barely utter the terrifying words. "Run, children! Run! Run away and be quick!"

In the pitch blackness of sight and sound, without the physical sensation of touch, all Amphytryon can do is float, despair, and hear the words of his old friends who stand outside in the courtyard.

Their old words come into Hercules' home and into Amphytryon's ears. "Listen, to the flute of death play the chant music of murder. Hercules is chasing his sons and hunting them down. Madness revels in frenzy rage inside the palace."

In the blackness of sight and sound, without physical sensations, Amphytryon floats in despair. The air inside the blood vessels inside his brain suffer from humidity. He cannot speak.

Ah! The worst of all miseries!

Floating in the darkness of sight and sound, without the ability to perceive physical sensations, and lacking the power of speech all Amphytryon can do is hear his friends in the courtyard outside.

Their words hang inside Hercules' home. "Old friends, lament for his old father. Groan for the mother who bore his babies and raised them in vain."

The humid air inside his blood vessels inside his brain have not impacted his hearing. The words from his old friends outside reach his ears loud and clear.

"Look! Look, there! A tempest quakes the building. The roof crashes down!"

"Hercules, son of Zeus, what are you doing? Hercules, you are sending a hellish confusion upon your house!"

"Goddess Athena once sent this hell's confusion upon the giant Enceladus!"

Enceladus? *The Titan who battled Athena during the Great War of Gods and Giants? He disgraced the meaning of his name "to sound the charge" when he fled the battlefield. His act of cowardice killed his own Typhoeus as a volcano crashed down. Why would my old comrades reference such a familial traitor? Oh Zeus! Why have you forsaken me?*

Murder, a Cruel Murder

The twenty old men have used their legs to run in circles and their lungs to scream. They act in an unmanly and unwarrior-like manner and have become women. Their feet feel the ground underneath quake and their eyes watch Hercules' home crash.

From the rubble, a middle-aged man emerges. He wears the uniform of a messenger. His eyes are wide open and show all the white. His mouth hangs. He wears the look of bewilderment. The group of old Theban warriors rush to the messenger's side and demand he speak and use words to describe what happened inside Hercules' home.

The messenger shouts the words. "Old men."

"Why speak so loudly?" The group of twenty old men stand still and stare. "Why shout?"

""Old men," the messenger wriggles his index finger in his ear, "there's a disastrous sight within the palace." He hangs his head low, shakes it from side to side, and then looks at the old men. His eyes frighten them His voice weeps.

The old men look at one another. They are impatient to learn what happened. "No prophet is needed to announce that."

"And there is no need to call another."

They want to hear the messenger speak the words. He looks at them and they see him collapse inside. "The children lie dead!"

Warrior men of old, who stood with spear and shield in hand, and fought for Thebes' survival begin to weep like boys who never lifted a stick. "A miserable thing!"

The messenger stumbles and wails about the courtyard. "Weep! This terror calls for loud weeping!"

"Murder, a cruel murder." The twenty old men crowd around the messenger. "Children killed by the murderous hands of their father."

The messenger looks at the old men one at a time. "Words can't be uttered." Each old man's eyes make contact before the messenger speaks again. "Descriptions won't match our suffering."

"Yet you must." The old men begin yelling. Some old men grab at the messenger's clothing. "Use words and descriptions."

"Explain this piteous ruin."

"Tell us clearly the path of father Hercules' destruction of outrage on his children."

The messenger looks at each of the twenty old men but his mouth won't open. They are anxious and impatient to understand the suffering and horror that took place inside Hercules' home.

"It raises our loudest sighs."

"Tell us how the heavens crashed down and came rushing upon his house."

"Say how the poor lives of his sons met their sad ending."

He has the Wolfish Rage!

Yes, Hercules! Kill the tyrant king.

Ha! Take that tyrant king's corpse. You can lay mutilated and disgraced outside the halls of Heracles' home.

Oh, thank Zeus, father of Hercules! Thank you for placing these children in the safe arms of your son, Hercules. It pleases my heart to see them around Zeus' altar surrounded by sacrificial victims. Hercules has used his strength to purify the palace.

Praise Zeus, father of Hercules! It is wonderful for these eyes to see his group of children, his wife Megara, and his old father stand around the altar like a lovely chorus. It pleases the heart that beats in my breast to see the holy basket of offerings passed in a holy circle around the altar.

Zeus, we will take a moment for reverential silence.

Wha..? What is Hercules, son of Zeus, doing? He was about to dip the torch in his right hand into the holy water. He stopped, without a word, and now stands in dumb-founded silence.

I am confused and disoriented. What should I do? His sons look at him wondering why their father takes so long.

The messenger maneuvers himself and sees that Hercules' face has changed. He looks distressed. His eyeballs are bloodshot and roll wildly in their sockets. His bearded cheek oozes with foam.

He has the wolfish rage!

His mouth dripping with foam, Hercules begins to speak in a frenzied way and laughs a madman's laugh. "Father, I won't perform this sacrifice until I have also killed Eurystheus."

Eurystheus? He wants to kill his cousin who lives in the city of Mycenae? But, we are far away in the city of Thebes?

"Why kindle a flame and perform a purification ritual twice? I do not need to toil twice. With one stroke, in a single move, I will fix both problems."

The wolfish rage has taken over! White foam falls from his mouth.

"I will kill Eurystheus and bring his head here. I will cleanse and purify my hands of those I've already killed. Spill the water, throw it away."

Oh! Hercules, son of Zeus, knocked over the holy water. After the rites were performed and the words were spoken. That won't please the gods.

"Rid your hands of the baskets."

He knocks holy baskets out of people's hands! Disgraceful!

"Somebody pass me my bow and arrows, and my club."

He has run out of the holy room to grab his weapons. Oh, Zeus protect us!

"I will travel to Mycenae with crowbars and pickaxes. I will tear down the iron foundations those Cyclope built with mason's hammers and Phoenician. I will heave them from their foundations with the city-walls."

What in the name of the demons that live in the underworld of Hades is Hercules doing? He is behaving as though he's walking to a chariot that doesn't exist. What? He is mounting a seat that didn't exist. What, now? He is striking and goading nonexistent horses. He pretends to hold a nonexistent whip in his fingers.

The messenger's eyes gaze at the people inside the room. He senses a twofold feeling inside the breasts of those around the altar.

Some of these people are half-amused and the other half fearful. No one knows whether to laugh or cry.

The messenger and the other people inside Hercules' home, stand close, and look at one another.

Has Hercules, son of Zeus, gone mad? Is he joking? Making sport?

The messenger, and the other people inside Hercules' house, dash about and try to evade Hercules. He runs around from one room in the palace to another. He finally stops in the center of the men's quarters.

Hades! The wolfish rage! He is saying he has arrived at the city of Nisus.

Hercules throws himself on the floor as though it were a feast table.

Hercules, son of Zeus, heroic half-mortal who came to save the land of Thebes, sits on the floor eating dirt!

Hercules' wide eyes look at the ground, his hands grab non-existent delicacies, and place them inside his foaming mouth. He waits a bit, then begins marching around the house.

"I am in the plains amid the wooded valleys of the Isthmus."

What is he saying?

"I will now wrestle in the Isthmus games."

His wolfish rage causes him to think he's in Corinth at some sort of Olympic games!

Hercules strips naked and begins wrestling a nonexistent opponent. He wrestles himself, switching from side to side, performing as both competitors. Then he stops.

Oh, Zeus! He acts the herald and proclaims himself victor!

Hercules is naked and his bearded face is covered in foam. His eyes are wide open and bulging. He begins calling on nonexistent spectators, telling them to be silent, and listen.

Hercules, son of Zeus! His sick mind makes him fancy he is in Mycenae.

Hercules shouts terrible and fearful threats against Eurystheus. His father grabs his son's stalwart and sturdy arm.

"My son, what is wrong? What do you mean by this strange behavior? Is your mind affected by the blood you've spilled?"

Hercules' mighty arm hits out at Amphitryon's hand and his mouth says the words, "Leave me be. You are Eurystheus' father. You will not save your child."

The wolfish rage! He thinks his own father is the father of his enemy. Oh, Zeus! What will your son do?

"I am not Eurystheseus' father. I am your father. These are your sons."

Hercules thrusts aside the hand he believes belongs to Eurystheus, brings arrows to his bow, and makes ready his quiver.

He thinks he's about to slay one of Eurystheus' sons.

His three sons - poor, frightened boys - rush and dart about. One clings to his hapless mother's garments. Another hides behind the shadow of a column. The third child cowers beneath the altar like a little bird.

"What are you doing?" Megara, the wife and mother, cries out. "You are their father? Why do you want to kill your own children?" She screams at Hercules.

His old father and all the servants also yell at him but he runs around the column. He hunts the child.

Such dreadful circles.

When he stands face to face with his son, he shoots him through the heart. The boy falls on his back. Blood first sprinkles then splashes on the stone pillars.

The boy gasps his last breath of life!

Hercules sees his son fall. "Triumph and joy." He boasts loudly, "Here lies one of Eurystheus' sons dead at my feet. Atoning for his father's hatred towards me."

Hercules turns toward his second son, crouching at the altar's base

He hopes to escape the slaughter!

Hercules aims his bow but before he can fire, the boy throws himself at his father's knees. "Do not slay me, father. Please do not kill me. I am your child." He flings his hand up to reach his father's beard. "I am your son. I am no son of Eurystheus. You are not going to kill his sons."

Hercules has a savage Gorgon-scowl. He turns his wild, monstrous gaze at his son.

Oh, no! Hercules realizes his son is too close to kill with a bow and arrow!

Hercules raises his club above his head and, like a blacksmith, hammers his boy's blond head.

He smashed his skull!

Hercules has now killed two of his boys and hunts for his third victim. The boy's mother quickly grabs him, runs off inside the rooms, and shuts all the doors behind her.

Oh, no! Hercules must believe he is in front of the Cyclops wall. Look at him digging under the door and using crowbars to lever them open.

When the door posts fall, Hercules kills both his wife and son with a single shaft from his bow. Hercules then runs off to look for his old father.

Athena

Athena! Oh, thank you for appearing while brandishing a sharp spear in your hand and wearing a plumed helmet.

The goddess Athena grabs a stone and hurls it at Hercules' chest. This stays his madness, calms his frenzied thirst for blood, and sends him plunging to sleep. He falls on the ground and hits his back on one of the fallen columns.

Time to Act

Now is our time to act!

"Come, brave men. Now that he is sleeping, let's tie him up."

The people inside the house of Hercules aid Amphitryon, his father, and bind Hercules in thick ropes with knotted cords.

"He is tied to the column so he won't do any more harm when he wakes."

"There the poor man sleeps."

"Not the best spot, the spot where he murdered his own children and wife."

For my part, that man is the most unfortunate and miserable mortal.

www.ingramcontent.com/pod-product-compliance
Lightning Source LLC
Chambersburg PA
CBHW081207170626
46811CB00011B/3332